After a While, Crocodile

Written by Melinda LaRose

Illustrated by Character Building Studio and the Disney Storybook Art Team

Disney PRESS
New York • Los Angeles

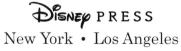

SUSTAINABLE FORESTRY INITIATIVE
Certified Chain of Custody
Promoting Sustainable Forestry
www.sfiprogram.org
SFI-01415
The SFI label applies to the text stock

Ahoy, mateys! Do you want to join my pirate crew? Then just say the pirate password: "Yo-ho-ho!" As part of my crew, you'll need to learn the Never Land pirate pledge.

TODAY'S PIRATE PLEDGE

A good pirate always helps a matey in need!

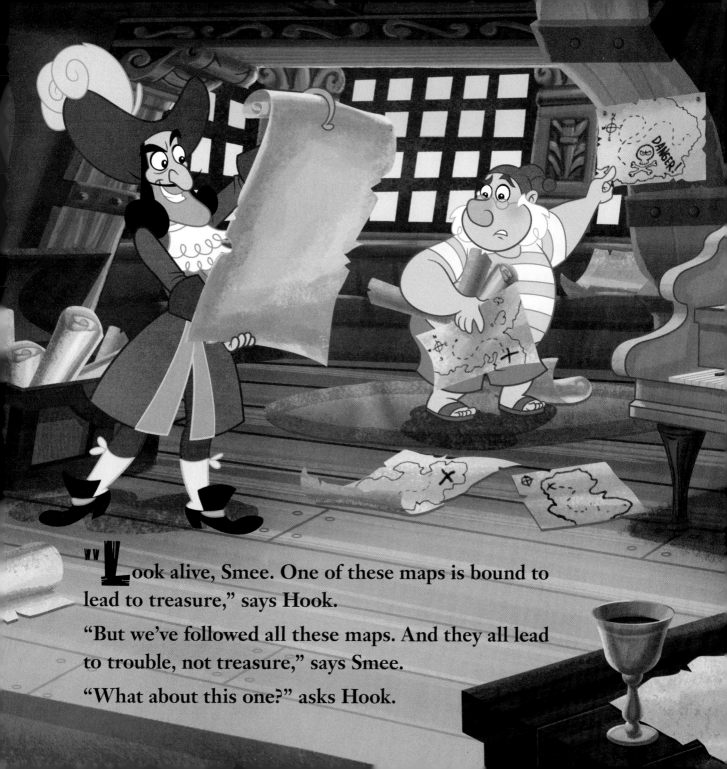

ook alive, Smee. One of these maps is bound to lead to treasure," says Hook.

"But we've followed all these maps. And they all lead to trouble, not treasure," says Smee.

"What about this one?" asks Hook.

"Oh, my," says Smee. "That treasure map leads to the biggest trouble of all—Crocodile Creek."

"**GULP!**" says Hook. "C-crocodile Creek? Home of the **T-TICK T-TOCK CR-CROC?**"

What time is it when the Tick Tock Croc comes to your house?

"I'm afraid so, sir," says Smee. "What do you say we have a nice, peaceful-like day polishing your hooks?"

"Never!" says Hook. "Croc or no Croc, I'm going to find that treasure!"

"Out of my way, puny pirates," says Hook. "Can't you see I'm looking for treasure?"

"But you're heading for Crocodile Creek," says Izzy.

"So what if I am?" asks Hook.

"AW, COCONUTS!" says Cubby. "There's a whole bunch of crocs in there!"

"Yeah, some treasures just aren't worth the trouble," says Jake.

"You just want me to give up so you can find the treasure yourself," says Hook. "Well, I'm not afraid of anything. Smee, you go first."

Time to run!

"Let's sneak in and out quick and quiet-like," says Smee.

Just then, Sharky and Bones start to sing a song:

"Captain Hook, he really rocks. Not afraid of a creek of crocs!"

"Stop that infernal singing!" shouts Hook. "You scurvy swabs will wake up all the crocs in the creek."

"We only woke up one crocky-dile," says Bones.

TICKTOCK! TICKTOCK!

SNAP!

"Crackers!" cries Skully. "The Croc just took a bite out of ol' barnacle britches' britches!"

"Hurry! We have to help Captain Hook," says Izzy.

"Here, boy! Fetch!" Jake throws a stick and the Tick Tock Croc chases after it.

"Now can we go back to the *Jolly Roger*?" asks Smee. "You might want to put on some pants."

I hope Hook has better luck finding pants than he has finding treasure.

"WAAA! OOF!" cries Hook. "What is this blasted net doing on the deck of me ship?"

"Sorry, Cap'n," say Sharky and Bones.

"Well? Don't just stand there. Get me out of it!" cries Hook.

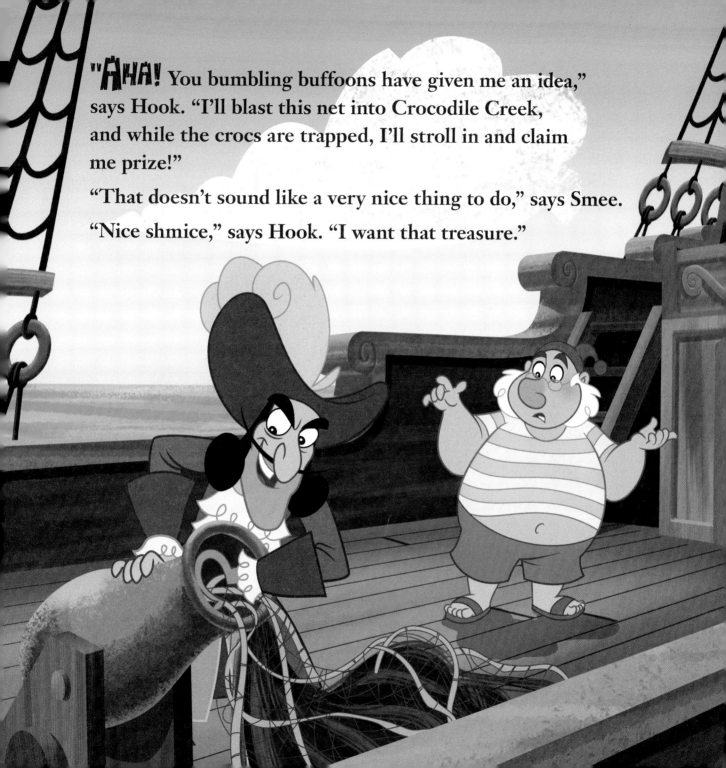

"**AHA!** You bumbling buffoons have given me an idea," says Hook. "I'll blast this net into Crocodile Creek, and while the crocs are trapped, I'll stroll in and claim me prize!"

"That doesn't sound like a very nice thing to do," says Smee.

"Nice shmice," says Hook. "I want that treasure."

Hook sails the *Jolly Roger* near Crocodile Creek.

"Ready? Aim! Fi—"

TICKTOCK! TICKTOCK!

"Shiver me timbers!" cries Smee. "There's a beastie aboard!"

Fwoom!

Smee accidentally fires the cannon and launches Hook into the sky.

"SAAAAAVE MEEEEE, SMEEEEEEE!" cries Hook.

Why did the pirate put his clock in the cannon?

"There's something you don't see every day," says Skully.
"A codfish in a tree."

"C'mon, mateys," says Jake. "Let's give the captain a hand."

"I'm on it." Skully untangles Hook from the net.

"Thank you, little birdies," says a dazed Captain Hook.

"Maybe it's time to call it a day and head back to the ship," suggests Jake.

"Never!" cries Hook as he falls over.

He wanted to see time fly!

Later Hook and Smee put on crocodile disguises to creep
and crawl through Crocodile Creek.

"What do I always say, Smee? If you can't beat 'em,
join 'em," says Hook.

"I've never heard you say that," says Smee.

"Oh, who asked you?" says Hook.

"I can't believe it. It's working," says Smee.
"I mean, brilliant plan as always, Cap'n."

Check out ol' Captain Croc!

"TREASURE AHOY," says Hook.

Smee accidentally steps on Hook's tail,
and the captain crawls right out of his costume.

"Those simple-minded crocs will never even know we
were here," says Hook.

"They're right behind me, aren't they?"

"**AY-EEEEEE!**" yells Hook. "Save me, Smee!"

"**YAY-HEY, NO WAY!**" says Izzy. "Every croc in the creek is after Captain Hook."

"This is an emergency," says Jake.

"Pixie Dust, away!" cries Izzy.

Why does the Croc keep chasing the captain?

Izzy sprinkles Hook and Smee with Pixie Dust, and the pirates soar into the sky.

"Up, up, and out of harm's way," laughs Smee. "Oh, thank you, little sea pup."

"I could've rescued meself," grumbles Hook.

Back on the *Jolly Roger*, Captain Hook can't wait to open his new treasure chest.

"Like I said, a few itty-bitty crocs are no match for Captain Hook."

Suddenly, Hook hears . . .

TICKTOCK!

TICKTOCK!

He's hooked on Hook!

"The beast is aboard me ship—again!" cries Hook.
"Abandon ship!"

"But, Cap'n . . ." starts Smee.

Hook jumps overboard even though the Tick Tock Croc
is nowhere in sight!

Captain Hook swims all the way to Pirate Island.

TICKTOCK! TICKTOCK! TICKTOCK!

"Ahhhh!" cries Captain Hook. "Hide me! The Tick Tock Croc is after me!"

"Whoa, there," says Jake. "There are no crocodiles around."

"There aren't?" asks Hook.

"The ticking is coming from your treasure chest," says Cubby.

Hook gasps! "Is it full of little Tick Tock Crocs?"

"I doubt it," says Jake. "But there's only one way to find out."

"Here. You open it," says Hook, handing Jake the chest.

Hook handing over treasure? Now I've seen everything!

"It's a golden alarm clock," says Jake.

"You mean the kind that goes *ticktock, ticktock* all day long?" asks Hook.

"That's the one," says Skully.

"You were right," says Hook. "Some treasures just aren't worth the trouble. You can have it!"

Brrriinnnng! The alarm goes off.

"AY-EEEEEE!" Captain Hook cries, running away.

"Thank you," calls Jake.

"Don't mention it," yells Hook, "ever again."

"Check it out! For helping Captain Hook steer clear of the Croc, we got eleven Gold Doubloons," says Jake. **"Yo-ho, way to go, mateys!"**

Don't be alarmed. I'll see you next time!